**For the baby I'm
carrying in my tummy.
J. C.**

The Library of Congress cataloged the prior edition as follows:

Library of Congress Cataloging-in-Publication Data

Cabrera, Jane.
Mommy, carry me please! / by Jane Cabrera.—1st ed. p. cm.
Summary: Various baby animals ask their mothers to carry them.
ISBN 978-0-8234-1935-5 (hardcover)
[1. Mother and child—Fiction. 2. Animals—Fiction.] I. Title.
PZ7.C1135Mo 2005
[E]—dc22
2004048862

ISBN: 978-0-8234-4474-8 (hardcover)

Mommy, Carry Me Please!

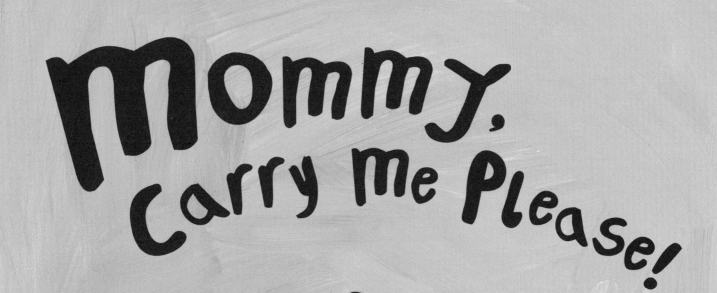

Jane Cabrera

HOLIDAY HOUSE · NEW YORK

Mommy Hippo,
carry me please
on your back
to keep me dry.

Mommy Crocodile,
carry me please
on your teeth
just for fun.

Mommy Penguin,
carry me please
on your feet
to keep me warm.

Mommy Lemur,
carry me please
next to your tummy
all fluffy and cozy.

Mommy Kangaroo,
carry me please
safe and snug
inside your pouch.

Mommy Tiger,
carry me please
in your mouth
to keep me safe.

Mommy Monkey,
carry me please
on your tail
as we play in the trees.

Mommy Beaver,
carry me please
on your head
to cross the river.

Mommy Koala,
carry me please
around your neck
to the top of the tree.

Mommy Spider,
carry me please
on your body
as you weave your web.

Mommy, Mommy,
carry me please . . .